SCOOBY-DOO!

MONKEY SEE MONKEY DOO

Written by Lee Howard
Illustrated by Alcadia SNC

Spotlight

ABDOPUBLISHING.COM

Reinforced library bound edition published in 2016 by Spotlight, a division of ABDO
PO Box 398166, Minneapolis, Minnesota 55439. Spotlight produces high-quality
reinforced library bound editions for schools and libraries. Published by agreement
with Warner Bros. Entertainment Inc.

Printed in the United States of America, North Mankato, Minnesota.
092015
012016

THIS BOOK CONTAINS
RECYCLED MATERIALS

CATALOGING-IN-PUBLICATION DATA

Howard, Lee.
Scooby-Doo in monkey see, monkey doo / Lee Howard.
    p. cm. (Scooby-Doo leveled readers)
Summary: A giant gorilla is causing problems at the zoo. Can Mystery, Inc. solve the problem
without any monkey business?
1. Scooby-Doo (Fictitious character)--Juvenile fiction. 2. Dogs--Juvenile fiction. 3. Mystery and
detective stories--Juvenile fiction. 4. Adventure and adventures--Juvenile fiction.
[Fic]--dc23
                    2015156080

978-1-61479-419-6   (Reinforced Library Bound Edition)

Spotlight

A Division of ABDO
abdopublishing.com

Scooby-Doo, Shaggy, and the gang arrived for a fun day at the zoo.

"Like, they have great snack stands here," Shaggy said. "Let's eat!"

"After we see some animals," said Daphne.

The gang headed straight to the big cat exhibit. One of the lions came over and roared at Scooby and Shaggy.

At the snack stand, Shaggy ordered a Zebra shake. Scooby got some Koala Krunchies.

"Like, m-m-m!" Shaggy said.

"Runchy," said Scooby.

"I want to see the monkeys," said Shaggy.

"Re, roo." Scooby made silly monkey sounds as they walked to the monkey house.

But the monkey exhibit was empty.

"Hey!" called Fred. "Where are all the monkeys?"

"Inside eating lunch?" said Velma. Suddenly, the zookeeper appeared. "At night something has been scaring the monkeys."

"Scaring them?" said Velma.

"And now they won't come out," the zookeeper explained. "I'm the new zookeeper, and I don't know what to do."

"Mystery, Inc. will investigate," said Velma. "Right, Scooby?"

"Ro ray!" Scooby cried.

"I think I have a plan…" Fred added.

"Ruh-roh," said Scooby.

"Like, I hear you, Scoob," Shaggy said. "Let's hope there's food involved."

Fred gathered the gang together. "Scooby and Shaggy will dress up as monkeys and stay with them," he began.

"Then we'll know who or what is scaring them," Velma said.

"And what's sure to scare Scoob and me," added Shaggy.

"Don't worry, guys," said Daphne. "We'll keep an eye on you."

"And you'll have fun playing with the other monkeys," Fred added.

Shaggy and Scooby went inside the monkey area.
"Roo!" cried Scooby. "Roo-roo!"

Fred, Daphne, and Velma watched.
"How will we see them in the dark?" Daphne asked.
"We'll use our night vision goggles," said Velma.
"They're in the Mystery Machine."

GROWL! "Like, my stomach's starving," said Shaggy.

Shaggy and Scooby looked at the monkeys' food.

Shaggy tried some. "Not bad."
Scooby helped himself. "Rummy!"
Suddenly they heard a sound.
"Wh-wh-what's that noise?" cried Shaggy.

A big shadow fell over Scooby and Shaggy. It waved its arms and reached for them with an angry GROWL!

"AHHHHHHH!" Scooby and Shaggy took off.

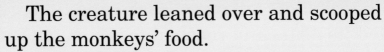

The creature leaned over and scooped up the monkeys' food.

"GRRRRRR!" It growled again and then ran away.

Velma and the others watched everything.
"Did you see the size of that thing?" said
Daphne.
"It might be a member of the gorilla
family," Velma said.

"We're gonna need a large net," Fred said.

"We have one in the Mystery Machine," said Velma.

"What else will we need?" Daphne asked.

"Boxes of Scooby Snacks," Fred said. "Lots of boxes," Velma said. "This creature is really hungry."

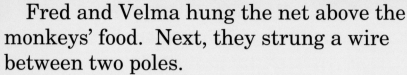

Fred and Velma hung the net above the monkeys' food. Next, they strung a wire between two poles.

"The creature will trip on the wire and the net will fall on him," said Fred.

"That should work," Velma said.

Meanwhile, Daphne made piles of Scooby Snacks. Then, she left a trail of snacks all around the monkey house.

"I hope Scooby doesn't eat everything before the creature comes back!" she said.

Fred, Velma, and Daphne hid behind some bushes in the monkey enclosure. "The creature should show up any time now," Fred whispered.

Suddenly, they saw something moving! Two figures were picking up Scooby Snacks. One was the creature; the other was Scooby!

The creature and Scooby bumped into each other. When they tripped on the wire, the net dropped on both of them!

"RAAAAA!" cried Scooby. "Relp!"

Scooby and Shaggy worked quickly to bag the creature.

"Got him!" they cried.

"Great job, guys," Fred said.

Scooby and Shaggy were making so much noise, the zookeeper came running out from the monkey house.

"What's going on?" the zookeeper asked.

Fred reached through the net and pulled off the creature's mask.

"Hey, you're the old zookeeper?" cried the new zookeeper.

The man nodded. "I wanted revenge for losing my job. I thought if I scared off the monkeys, no one would come to the zoo," he said.

With the mystery solved, Shaggy and Scooby joined their new friends for a breakfast of bananas and monkey business! "Scooby-Dooby-Doo!"